Tales of the Were
Grizzly Cove

Saving
Grace

BIANCA D'ARC

This book is a work of fiction. The names, characters, places, and incidents are products of the writer's imagination or have been used fictitiously and are not to be construed as real. Any resemblance to persons, living or dead, actual events, locale or organizations is entirely coincidental.

No part of this book may be used or reproduced in any manner whatsoever without written permission, except in the case of brief quotations embodied in critical articles and reviews.

DEDICATION

With deepest thanks to my friends and family, for putting up with me.

Special thanks to my editor, Jess, and the rest of the team, and sincerest thanks to the readers who make this all possible. Especially my facebook friends, Anna-Marie, Tina, Tamara, Grace, Lisa, Stacy, Tracie, Barbara, and so many others who make each day fun. Love you guys!

CHAPTER ONE

Jack liked the solitude of being outdoors, away from people, especially in the winter. Regardless, he always made at least a few appearances each month at his brother's house, which was usually filled with his new sister-in-law's family and their mates. The ladies liked to organize family meals every weekend, which was something Jack and his brother, Brody, hadn't experienced since before leaving home.

Things in the cove had been simpler when it had been just the guys from their old military unit. All single. But now, four of Grizzly Cove's residents were mated, including Brody, and the Alpha, John.

Things had changed drastically in the cove, and while it was a happy time for the newlyweds, the rest of them were all on alert because of the threat still coming from the water. The creature known as the leviathan was waiting, a mostly unseen menace, watching and waiting to pounce, given the slightest opening.

John's new mate, Ursula, was a powerful witch. She had nearly died placing magical wards to keep the leviathan out of the cove itself and away from shore, for the most part, but there was still a problem. The evil creature was still out there, waiting for any break in their defenses to feed upon the power of anyone caught out, away from the safety of the wards.

The leviathan and its army of smaller minions kept trying to break through the wards and encroach closer to the cove, but so far, they'd been unsuccessful. Better safe than sorry, though, so all the residents of the cove had decided to stay vigilant.

Which was why Jack was out here, walking the shoreline after dark, doing his job as Game Warden of Grizzly Cove. The title was mere ceremony, as were most of the officious-sounding job titles given to the former military members of the growing community. Their real function was as guards, lookouts, spies and peacekeepers. Goddess knew, they'd acted in all those capacities during their time working for Uncle Sam. Now they were using those hard-earned skills to protect and defend their new town.

There had been real trouble a few weeks back, before the wards had been placed. Deputy Zak Flambeau's new mate had been attacked right on the beach by a tentacled creature trying to drag her into the water. Only Zak's ferocious claws had been able to stop it. He'd shredded the tentacle, which was now resting in a refrigerator in the back of the town hall, parts of it having been taken by courier for further examination by specialists.

Nobody had known what the heck the animal was, but it had reeked of magic. Black magic. Not friendly in the least. After that, the water, and most of the beach, had been declared off limits, but only the lone polar bear in town seemed to mind. He actually liked swimming in temperatures that would freeze the balls off any other *normal* bear, the crazy son of a bitch.

Jack had gone all the way around the cove on his rounds, checking the perimeter and making sure all was well in the woods and beach that bordered their little town. He was up by the southern tip of the cove, where the land met the sea, almost at the end of his rounds. His house wasn't too far away, which was why he began and ended his scouting of the perimeter from this point each evening. He liked the isolation of living on the edge of the ocean. Something about the waves he could see from his hilltop home called to him, though he didn't really understand why.

Just a few more minutes and he'd be able to go home and clean up in time to head over to his brother's place. Family dinners were sort of mandatory now that Brody had claimed a mate. Jack didn't begrudge him that. He really liked his new sister-in-law. But Jack and Brody had never really been as close as some of the other siblings in their group. They'd been born a generation apart, and Jack was more of a loner, preferring to spend time in the woods—either in his fur or out of it—more than with other people.

Which was probably why they'd given

him the job of Game Warden when they were passing out titles and duties. Their Alpha, John, knew each of the men too well to give them a job for which they weren't suited. Settling in Grizzly Cove was supposed to be a reward, not a punishment, so John was sure to give each of the guys a choice if they wanted to work in a job or not. Most were content to serve the community they were all trying to build, in one way or another.

Jack was happiest on his own, and observing nature—and potential threats from humans, shifters, or Others—was his specialty. So his job was a near-perfect fit.

Stepping over a rise in the dunes, well away from the danger that might possibly be lurking in the water, Jack looked out over the expanse of rocky sand toward the shoreline. His night vision was excellent, but he had to squint to be sure he was seeing what he thought he was seeing.

Sure enough, there was a crumpled shape lying on the sand not far from the receding waterline. The tide was going out, and it looked like something—or someone—had washed up on the beach. Was it alive? Was it a trap to get him closer to the water?

Only one way to find out.

Jack approached cautiously, but with some speed. If it was a trap, he didn't want to give the enemy time to plan every move. It was better to rush the scene, Jack thought, though others might've disagreed with his tactics. Of course, Jack had always been a bit unconventional. For a bear, he was a bit of a lone wolf at times.

As he drew closer, he could see pale skin that had an almost luminous glow. And the red of blood. The coppery scent hit him as the breeze shifted, and he knew that whatever it was on the beach was gravely injured. Maybe even dead.

But no. He saw the faint rise and fall of breathing as he got closer. It was alive. For now.

And…female, he saw, as he got closer. But she was like no female he'd ever seen before. That glow was the fading of what could only be described as scales. And as he watched, her lower body dried and became two legs instead of a single, thick tail.

Holy shit.

He'd found himself a mermaid.

Her breathing was labored, and Jack could see all kinds of cuts, bruises and lacerations on her naked body. The fact that she was absolutely gorgeous didn't escape his notice, but at the moment, he was more concerned about keeping her alive. She was in bad shape.

Throwing caution to the wind, he went right up to her and lifted her off the cold, gritty sand. He had to get her someplace safe where her wounds could be tended. The closest safe place was his house, and Jack didn't hesitate. He strode off quickly toward his home, never once looking back at the raging ocean and giant, angry tentacles waving around in the distance behind him.

Oh, Jack knew the creature was there. It was probably the very same creature that had chomped Master Hiram's yacht to little splinters a few weeks ago, but Jack figured it couldn't come any closer to shore because of the wards.

The mermaid had probably escaped the big creature either by being caught up in the current and washed ashore accidentally, or by deliberately beaching herself to escape. Either way, the wards had probably saved her life. Jack would take it from there and make sure she lived to tell the tale.

He was also fascinated by the idea of

entertaining a mermaid in his home. Until tonight, he hadn't been sure they even existed. Now he knew. He had the living proof in his arms.

CHAPTER TWO

Grace was warm and stationary, which wasn't right. The ocean was cold and ever moving. Why was she on dry land? Something was wrong…

Grace fought against the fog that tried to keep her unconscious, battling through the layers of pain and confusion to burst through the surface of sleep into wakefulness, and found herself…in a soft bed, in a lovingly decorated room that looked like it was part of the forest itself.

Muted greens and browns dominated with accents of gray and tan. The furniture was like nothing she'd ever seen before. Twisted tree limbs and knotted pine had been shaped into the bed frame, chair and matching table. A simple lamp sat on the table, along with a pitcher of water and a glass.

Water. That would help her more than anything.

Grace reached for it, and had to stifle a moan as she moved. She paused to take stock before she tried for the water again.

Under the green comforter, she found bandages. Lots and lots of bandages. And someone had dressed her in a long white shirt. A man's shirt, though, on her, it was big enough to be a dress.

She did an internal inventory and realized she must've been on land for several hours at least. She was dry almost to the point of being parched. Sucking in a breath and steeling herself, she reached again for the pitcher and glass.

"Let me get that for you," a deep voice said from the doorway. She looked up, caught in the deep brown gaze of the most handsome man she'd ever seen. Sandy brown hair topped his tall frame. He was long and lean, muscular without being overly so, and his dark eyes sparkled with life and intelligence.

He moved closer and picked up the pitcher, pouring her half a glass of water. He handed it to her, and she raised it to her lips, but she was at a bad angle. She tried to sit up and groaned at the pain in every limb.

"I'll help you. Just hang on," the man said, moving closer.

He grabbed some pillows off the chair at the side of the bed and put one broad hand behind her back, lifting her. With his other hand, he stuffed a few pillows behind her, supporting her with gentle touches while he helped her sit up.

She lifted the glass to her lips again and, this time, was successful in sipping. She tried to be ladylike—remembering her land manners—but she was too thirsty. She downed the entire glass and held it out for more.

Understanding dawned in the man's eyes. "Wait a sec. I have an idea."

He picked up a paper-wrapped straw that had been sitting on the bedside and unwrapped it. Sliding the straw into the pitcher, he brought the entire thing to her, placing it in her lap.

"Are you okay with this?" he asked, helping her hold it, probably wondering if she was strong enough to do it herself.

She held up one finger while sucking on the straw. As thirsty as she was, he wasn't going to have to wait long to take the pitcher away. Empty.

Sure enough, after a few intense moments of sucking water through the straw, Grace was starting to feel better. She allowed the straw to make noises along the bottom of the pitcher as she sucked up the last of the water, then she released it and looked up at him.

"More, please?" she whispered, not sure how her voice was going to sound.

Much to her surprise, it was all right. She hadn't spent a lot of time on land since leaving San Francisco, but she did talk with her sister occasionally above the surface. She'd screamed her throat raw when the monster attacked, though, and it still felt very sore. Luckily, it seemed like she hadn't lost the use of her voice completely.

"You can have all you want, ma'am," the man said politely, lifting the pitcher and moving toward another doorway in the room she hadn't noticed before.

He opened it, and she realized it was a bathroom. The tub looked large, and it had a shower too. She heard the water running in the sink, and a few minutes later, he returned with the pitcher full again.

"Do you want it now, or shall I just pour you a glass and leave the rest on the table?" he asked solicitously. He seemed a little nervous around her, though he was very polite. In all likelihood, he had saved her life.

"Just a glass, thank you. And my name is Grace," she told him. "Thank you for rescuing me. Did you find me on the beach?"

"I did. You were cut up pretty bad," he said, frowning a bit. "Sea monster trouble, right?"

"How did you know?" She'd thought none of the land dwellers realized what had come to their shores, but maybe she was wrong.

"The big one ate the Master vampire of Seattle's yacht a few weeks ago. He survived, but he wasn't happy. And then, a smaller version of the creature attacked my friend's mate. It wrapped a tentacle around her leg and tried to drag her into the cove, but my buddy fought it off."

"He must be quite the warrior to have defeated such a creature," she said, impressed.

"Zak? Yeah, he's okay, even if he is smaller than the rest of us."

"Smaller?" She wondered how large these men were if the smallest one could take on one of those creatures and prevail.

The man took a seat on the chair and met her gaze. "He's a black bear. Most of us are grizzlies." She was impressed that he was speaking so openly about their differences. If he was talking so freely, he must realize... "And you're a mermaid."

His gaze held hers.

"Something like that," she admitted, feeling her cheeks heat with embarrassment, though she had no idea why she should be embarrassed. Although... "It's been a long time since anyone on land knew what I was."

"Well..." He sat back, looking only marginally less threatening. He was a *big* man. "You're safe here. Most everyone in this town is a shifter. Mostly bears of different varieties, though grizzlies outnumber the others. We have a few select humans who are mated to some of my colleagues. And a lot of us are ex-military.

Special Forces. We can protect you."

"On land, maybe," she muttered.

"Yeah, sorry about that. We've got a call in to some specialists, but they can't come right away. They're busy on the other side of the world and out of com range, but when they finish their mission, we've been promised they'll come help with our little sea monster problem."

"What kind of specialists? Some sort of water-based shifters? I have to tell you, they won't have much luck. That thing is unlike anything I've ever seen before, and it reeks of evil."

"We have connections with a couple of water sprites—well, descendants of a water sprite and a human. They're Navy SEALs."

Grace was impressed and didn't mind that her face probably showed it. He'd been pretty up front with her, and she wasn't getting any bad vibes off him. He seemed honest and exactly as he claimed. She had no reason—yet—to doubt his words, though she would be wary. She'd been warned that land dwellers weren't always as straight-forward as those in the sea.

"Sprites might have a chance," she admitted. "They'd need a lot of magic to go up against that thing."

"Do you know what it is?" he asked quietly.

She shook her head. "Evil. That's all I know. As I said, I've never seen anything like it before, and I pray I never see its like again."

"The witches we know think it's a leviathan—an evil creature from another realm, brought here by servants of the Destroyer of Worlds."

"I can believe that. It's pretty awful."

"We have wards on the land that reach a short way off the beach, but we didn't know there were any magical folk out there, like you, who might run afoul of the things once we pushed them back. I know we didn't intend to cause you trouble."

"I think I felt the ward when I crossed it, and the creature couldn't follow. I was badly injured by then and let the tide take me, since it was pulling me away from the monster." She thought for a moment. "We've all known something wasn't right for a while. I don't think your wards caused it to get worse."

"It cut you up pretty badly," he said after a short pause. "I did my best to bandage your wounds, but I wasn't sure what special care you might require. Can I get you anything that will help you heal faster?"

"Just keep the water flowing," she replied, lifting the glass and draining it. She placed it back on the bedside table, and he refilled it from the pitcher. "I didn't expect to live through that encounter. I think you probably saved my life, and for that, I thank you."

He held up his hands, palms outward. "No need. I'm just glad I was there to help. My name is Jack Chambers, by the way. I'm the cove's Game Warden."

She had to smile at that. "Looks like you found more than you bargained for washed up on your beach last night."

He smiled back, and she loved the way his eyes crinkled up at the corners, as if he smiled a lot. He really was the most handsome man.

"You've got that right. And when you're feeling up to it, the Alpha would like to talk to you." He stood and gave her a small black remote control. That disarming smile of his made her heart beat a little faster.

"The remote is labelled pretty well, but ask me if you need anything. The TV will pop up if you push that blue button, and I've got a satellite on the roof, so lots of channels to choose from. There's also a selection of music and intercom access if you want to find me. See the orange button?"

He pointed it out, and she was impressed by the level of technology in his otherwise rustic-looking home. She hit the blue button, and a large black screen rose from inside the opposite wall and turned on to a news channel.

"I haven't seen television in a long time. Thank you. I'll familiarize myself with what's been going on ashore." Scenes of an explosion half a world away distracted her while he stood.

"If you're okay, then I'll be back in a bit. Just hit the orange button if you want anything."

"Will do. Thank you, Jack," she said, watching a fiery crash on the television as he walked out.

CHAPTER THREE

Jack dialed John's number as he walked out into the main part of his home. The Alpha picked up on the first ring.

"Sitrep," was John's short greeting. All Alpha. Always in charge. But Jack didn't mind. John was a good leader and had never steered any of them wrong.

"She's awake," he told John. "Nice girl. Currently watching TV in my guest room."

"Does she have any intel on the leviathan?"

"Not really. She said it was evil, but she claims never to have seen anything like it before. I believe her. She has no reason to withhold information."

"That you know of," was John's skeptical answer.

"Yeah, okay. You got me there. But you didn't see her injuries, John. She told me she didn't expect to live through the encounter, and if I hadn't come along, I don't think she'd have made it 'til morning. That thing sliced her up bad."

"I've got to make the rounds, but I'll come by later today. Keep her there."

"I don't think she'll be going anywhere today, but if she wants to take her chances back in the ocean, I can't, in good conscience, keep her here against her will. I will strongly suggest that she shouldn't return to the water, but I won't hold her prisoner." There were some things at which Jack drew the line.

"Understood," John replied. He didn't sound happy about it, but Jack knew the Alpha really did understand the need to give any magical creature its freedom. "I'll see you in a while."

Jack hung up and peeked in the door to find Grace's eyes closed. She was asleep again, poor gal. He figured she needed the rest, so he slipped quietly away and headed toward the kitchen. He'd prepare some food for when she woke again. Maybe something salty. And liquidy. Soup was a good bet. He probably had a can of the condensed stuff somewhere that he could start with.

He was just finishing making the soup when he heard the pitter patter of bare feet on his hardwood floors. She was up? He hadn't thought she'd be out of bed before tomorrow, at the earliest, but then again, what did he know about mermaids? Maybe they healed faster than he'd guessed.

Jack turned to find her standing uncertainly in the archway to the kitchen.

"I'm surprised you're up. How do you feel?" He tried to put her at ease, but she looked decidedly uncomfortable standing there in his shirt that came down to her knees.

She was totally *hot* too. Her long, dark hair had dried to a wavy chestnut, and her unforgettable eyes were the color of cool, pure water. A bright aqua blue so pale they almost looked like crystal.

But the uncertainty on her face made him want to comfort rather than pounce. Maybe he'd get to pounce later. Or maybe not. Either way, he wanted her to feel welcome in his home—unless and until she proved to be something other than the innocent she looked.

"A little shaky," she admitted with a tiny smile. "Is that soup?"

"Chicken noodle, with some added veggies. Nothing fancy, but they say chicken soup is good when you're healing. Want some?" He turned back to the stove, already grabbing the ladle and pot. He'd put out a bowl earlier, intending to make up a tray for her.

"Sure," she agreed and sat at the kitchen table while he spooned soup into the bowl.

He set up another bowl for himself and joined her at the table a few minutes later. She was already sipping at the hot liquid, her face radiant, her eyes closed as she savored each bite. Jack felt a warm glow of satisfaction fill him. He'd guessed right on what to make for her.

"This is great. It's been a long time since I had land food. Everything we eat below is cold. And raw," she added. "But I guess you probably understand. You eat in your shifted form, right?"

"Yeah, my inner bear likes to hunt," he agreed. It was new to have this sort of

22

conversation with a woman. All of his lovers in the past had been human and, therefore, uninformed about his true nature. It was oddly refreshing to be able to be open with Grace about his other form.

"My mer form may not look like as full of a shift as yours, but it probably is. I have scales everywhere, and even though I can still speak with my mouth above water, I don't often do so. We tend to live rather solitary lives, hunting in our own territories, gathering only rarely with family."

"Sounds a lot like us. Most bears are solitary. This town is a big experiment."

"Why?" She took a sip of her soup, then clarified. "Why gather so many shifters in one place? Why are you doing it?"

Jack thought about how to answer. "There are a few different reasons. For one thing, we were all ready to retire. We spent a lot of years fighting human wars, and the core group of us formed strong bonds. We didn't want to disband completely, which is what probably would have happened if our Alpha hadn't come up with this idea."

"You mentioned you were a warrior?" Grace asked, looking genuinely interested.

"Soldier. Special Forces," he clarified.

"We all were. A bunch of bear shifters gathered together under one leader, which is very unusual for our kind, but John doesn't take himself too seriously, which is good, and he's also a master of strategy. Like I said, he came up with this plan to build the town. He bought up most of the land very quietly during his years in the military and had it all ready to go when we'd all had enough. He cleared everything with the Native humans who live just to the south, and came up with our cover story too."

"Which is?" she asked, arching one eyebrow as she smiled over her spoon.

Jack had to smile back. "Believe it or not, we're an artists' colony. Each of us is expected to produce some kind of art or craft and put it up for sale in the galleries in town. That's our cover, and so far, the few humans who trek through here have bought it—and the crap we put in the galleries too." He shook his head, still not quite believing it.

"So what's your art form?"

He shifted in his seat a little uncomfortably, but he'd started this conversation, so he had to fess up.

"I make furniture out of saplings and tree limbs," he admitted, feeling a bit sheepish.

"Oh!" Her eyes went round in surprise. "All the lovely furniture in my room! I feel like I'm sleeping in the forest. I was admiring it when I woke up. And you made all that?"

"Everything in the house, actually." He scratched the back of his neck, feeling unaccountably flushed.

She paused to look around, running her hand over the smooth wood of the table, then bending to look underneath at the supports he'd made out of tree stumps. Then she looked at the chair and whatever else she could see of the place. Jack felt his skin crawl. What did she think of his den? He'd never really shown it to anyone—especially a female—before. It was still a bit of a work in progress in spots, in fact.

"You built the house too, didn't you?" She looked up at the exposed rafters high above.

"Guilty as charged."

"It's beautiful, Jack. Really in tune with the nature around it. I can tell." She went back to her soup, leaving him wondering exactly what she meant. She hadn't seen it from the outside. She'd been unconscious when he brought her in.

"How can you tell?" He was curious

25

enough to ask.

She looked up at him. "Oh. I can feel it. Vibrations travel differently through air, but I can still feel the forest's satisfaction with the structure you have put within its sheltering boughs."

Jack was fascinated by the idea. "I like the way you put that. It's probably the nicest thing anyone's ever said about my building skills."

He would've said more and asked more questions, but his phone vibrated, alerting him to someone approaching from the small rural road they'd run out to the edge of the cove. He'd put sensors out there since traffic was so light. He had more sensors all through his plot of land too, but in this case, he was expecting John, the Alpha.

"We're about to have company," Jack said, rising from his seat and heading toward the front door. "The Alpha has come out to meet you."

"Oh." She looked a little alarmed.

"Don't worry. He just wants to check you out and make sure you're on the right side. He's responsible for who we let into our territory, and it's his job to be careful." He saw her face pale, and he cursed his lack of eloquence. "It'll be okay, Grace. I know you're on the level, and he'll figure that out within moments of meeting you." He placed one hand on her shoulder, squeezing gently in what he hoped she would take as a reassuring gesture. "Sit tight. I'm going to let him in."

He saw her visibly gulp, but there was nothing he could do about her nervousness. He kicked himself for causing it. He shouldn't have said anything. *Dammit.*

Jack stalked toward the door and threw it open less than graciously as John approached. John shot him a look, but Jack ignored it. He wanted to get back to Grace and make sure she didn't bolt because he'd frightened her.

"Come on in. She's in the kitchen," he said shortly, leaving John to close the door while Jack went ahead, going back to the kitchen.

He cursed himself again when he found Grace leaning heavily against the back of the chair, standing with the table between them, a look of extreme fear on her face. He slowed his steps and approached her as gently as he could.

"It's okay, sweetheart. John just wants to

meet you. If he pulls any shit, I'll throw him out on his ass. Promise." Jack was deliberately blunt, hoping to spark a smile out of her, or at least a show of confidence in his ability to protect her. But neither was forthcoming as John entered the kitchen behind him.

"You might try, but I doubt you'd succeed," John said dryly. "Ma'am." Jack looked back to find John nodding respectfully at Grace. "I'm John Marshall."

"Grace Waters," she replied, still trying to stand her own, but Jack could see it was costing her.

"For Goddess' sake, sit down, both of you. She's just out of her sick bed and probably shouldn't be up and around at all yet," Jack groused, standing at the side of the table, between them.

"Please, Ms. Waters, sit down so we can too," John said politely, even going so far as to crack a smile.

Grace looked skeptical, but she retook her seat, keeping wary eyes on John.

CHAPTER FOUR

"Do you serve the Goddess?" the Alpha bear asked in a low, stern voice.

Grace felt compelled to answer, even though that question had hit her totally out of left field. She had expected something completely different. Not an inquiry into her spiritual beliefs.

Just what kind of shifters were these bears, after all?

"We of the sea are different from you land dwellers. Neptune is real. He rides the currents in his seahorse-drawn chariot. We fear him, but we revere the Light. Some of my selkie friends worship the Goddess of which you speak. We simply serve the Light, though there are those in the deeps who worship evil and dwell in perpetual darkness." She frowned. "We steer clear of them as best we can. It's a very big ocean, and there are relatively few of us."

"What happened to you that washed you up on our shore?" The Alpha went on, a bit more compassion in his tone.

"I didn't see the entirety of the creature you call the leviathan, but it's huge. Larger than the largest whale I know. And it seethes with anger. Its limbs roil the water and raise clouds of sand and debris wherever it is, which is why I couldn't see much of it. It felt like the tentacles just came out of nowhere at me." She cringed, remembering those horrible impacts. "Each blow propelled me through the water, and I tried to swim as fast as I could away, but it pursued."

"How did you get away?" Jack asked. She saw concern in his eyes, and she was instinctively drawn to him.

"I made for the shore, thinking it couldn't pursue me there. It was too fast to out-swim. I finally reached a point where I felt your ward as I passed through and realized the creature couldn't come any closer. It was repulsed by the ward. And then, the tide took me, and the next thing I knew, I woke up here."

John frowned, steepling his fingers together on the table in front of him. "Ms. Waters," he began, seeming to be searching for words. "I don't know how much Jack's already told you about our town, so let me nutshell it for you. We're a community of shifters. Bears, mostly. And among land-based shifters, bears are some of the most magical. Usually, we don't congregate together in such large numbers. This town is sort of a social experiment. We've become aware of the possibility that concentrating this much magic in one area might have attracted the creature—whatever it is—to our shore. We've already warned all our people. We've also contacted specialists, and we've been promised help, but our best bet is to just keep everyone out of the water for now."

"Yet my kind live in the water," she said, her voice filled with sadness. She missed the ocean, but she didn't want to die there. Not anytime soon, at any rate.

"You can't live on land?" Jack asked, frowning.

"Oh, we can," she replied. "We just mostly stay in the ocean these days unless we have a reason to be ashore. It's simpler. Land dwellers aren't as used to magic as they once were. I grew up on land, though, with my mother and father. Dad's human, and Mom is still with him. They live in San Francisco. I visit often, but I've been learning the ways of my ocean sisters for the past twenty years or so. They tell the neighbors I work in Tokyo."

She smiled at the subterfuge. Her family was small but perfect and full of love.

"We live probably as long as you do," she added. "And Mom was able to give Dad some of her magic so they can be together as long as possible. That happens with true mates like them."

"That's good to know," the Alpha said, sitting back in his chair. "I assume there are more of your people out there, off shore."

It wasn't a question, and she didn't want to betray specific information to this unknown leader of bears, but she would trust him...a little.

"We live and work in small groups— hunting parties are the most common. Some larger ones exist—shoals and pods. I am part of a hunting party. I think the rest of my group are probably worried about me by now, though we often go off on our own to scout. That's what I was doing when I ran into the leviathan."

"And do they all serve the Light, as you do?" the Alpha asked, his expression again serious.

She couldn't understand why they were so hung up on religion. She needed to know more about that before she could tell them any more about her people.

"We do, but why are you so concerned about our beliefs? I don't understand." She figured she'd try the honest approach first and see what the bears did.

The Alpha blinked a few times. "I guess you don't know about the problems we've been having up here on land."

"Grace, shifter groups all over the world have been under attack by agents of the *Venifucus*. Do you know who they are?" Jack said gently, his gaze concerned.

Chills ran down her spine.

"I've heard of them, but…" She cast through her memories of history lessons from her youth. "They're supposed to be over with. Gone. Disbanded when their leader was banished to the farthest realm. Our people were involved with the battle against Elspeth back then. I think that's probably the last time we mixed freely with land-dwelling Others in any great numbers."

Both men sighed, and the sounds weren't happy.

"They're back," Jack said, practically spitting the words. "They've been quietly regrouping these past years and planning ways to bring their leader back. Several attempts have been foiled over the past few years, but they keep trying. According to our sources, they've even infiltrated the *Altor Custodis* organization, using information from the watchers' files to target shifters and Others they think will try to stand in their way. Many innocents have already died."

"That's awful." A sense of dread came over her with each of his words.

The presence of the sea monster was starting to make more sense now. If evil was trying to return to this world, its minions would be the forerunners. That creature had to be one of those.

"I didn't know," she told the men. "Word of this hasn't reached us beneath the waves. I doubt my parents know. They keep to themselves and don't mix with Others. But it might explain a few things."

"Like the monster in the ocean, perhaps?" the Alpha asked astutely.

When she met his gaze, he was smiling, just slightly.

"Exactly what I was thinking. When evil forces stir, the creatures that do well in such an atmosphere grow bolder. Or so I've been taught." She understood now why they were so insistent on knowing what side she was on in the perpetual fight of good against evil. "I'd like to call my mother and warn her, if that's okay."

"Certainly," the Alpha answered right away. "I've also been wrestling with the question of what to do if more of your folk wish to come ashore until the danger is past."

He left his thoughts open-ended, possibly wanting her to offer an opinion. She didn't know exactly what to say, but she did know where to begin.

"Alpha, please let me set your mind at ease on one point at least. Mer do not generally seek to align ourselves with evil. There may be the isolated group or individual here and there, just like in any population, but mostly, we are peaceful sea dwellers. When we are shifted, our animal nature is very strong. I'm not sure how it is for you, but we tend to be very all or nothing. Hunt or play. Fight or sleep. Black or white. Good or evil. The mer form is very interested in survival in the ocean currents and finding its next meal."

"So is the bear, most of the time," Jack agreed, nodding. "The animal side is more primal than the human side."

"But how much does the beast side control when you are in its form? I've heard it's different for land dwellers than for us in the sea. For me, the mer is definitely running the show, since the human side of me wouldn't really know how to survive in the open ocean for long. I'm like a passenger in my own body while the mer is in charge, and it's the opposite when I'm on land."

Jack's eyebrows drew together in a tiny frown as he thought about her words.

"I wouldn't describe it like that for me. The bear is always there, in the back of my mind. He's listening in right now, watching, hearing, evaluating scents, reading body language, and offering his own insights. And when I'm furry, I'm still me. The human side

36

is present in the shifted form, helping the beast side make decisions and recognize things about the human world the beast doesn't always understand."

She was starting to understand the differences. The knowledge gave her new insight.

"Alpha…" She was about to reveal information about her friends and family. She hoped she was doing the right thing. "My hunting party will mostly likely be looking for me. If they follow my trail, they'll probably find the same evil that found me. I can vouch for every member of my group. They are all creatures of good intentions who serve the Light. I would ask that if any of my group come ashore, that you would render aid, as Jack has done for me. Please."

The Alpha sat up straight and looked her in the eye.

"I'll do more than that, Ms. Waters. My instincts tell me to trust you, but for the sake of the town, I'll ask you to stay with Jack here, for the next few days, at least. I'm going to offer you—and any like you who wish it—asylum here in Grizzly Cove, for as long as you need it. I'm doing this on my own authority, but I'll bring it before the town council and let them know what's going on. To that end, I'd like you to come to one of our meetings so they can see you and ask you a few questions. When you're up to it, of course. Not right away. I'll break the news to them and tell everyone to be on the lookout for any mer that might be in distress."

"Thank you," Grace said, her words choked with emotion.

"You're doing the right thing, John," Jack told his Alpha. "You can tell them you've got my vote of support."

Grace looked at Jack, realizing what his words must mean. "You're on the town council?"

Jack smiled at her. "The town council is just a fancy name for the guys in our old unit. We all have a vote in what goes on in this town."

John stood and smiled at her too. "I may be the Alpha, but I'm not a despot. Bears aren't so easily led. We're a little too independent to just follow anyone blindly. The position of Alpha is more ceremonial among us than other species."

"John is the Alpha because he's probably the smartest of us," Jack said, giving his friend a compliment. "He's also really good at paperwork." They both chuckled at that. "But we all get a say in the big decisions."

Grace was impressed. She'd thought land-dwelling shifters used more of a hierarchy and deferred to their Alphas uniformly. From their words, it sounded like there were differences in how each of the different kinds of shifters worked their groups.

"Well..." John said, resting his hands on the back of the wooden chair, looking at her. "That's all, really. I just wanted to meet you and get a read on your beliefs. My bear is a pretty good judge of character, and he likes you. You can thank my furry side for offering sanctuary to you and your people. He and I both know what it's like to have no clear line of retreat. We're offering you one. Here. With us. You can stay until it's safe again for you in the ocean."

She tried to stand, but her knees were too weak. Jack placed his hand over hers on the table. She met his gaze, and he was shaking his head, frowning at her. She gave up trying to move and just looked up at the Alpha.

"Thank you. For myself and for my people. I don't know if any of them will wash ashore like I did, but if they do, I'm glad to know they'll be welcome here. It's a dark day, indeed, when even the vast ocean isn't safe."

She thought quickly about how to get the word out to her people beneath the waves.

"I know there are at least two fishing boats that leave your cove most days," she began hesitantly, still thinking through the possibilities. "I'm not sure how, but maybe, if your men still insist on fishing, there might be a way to get word to my hunting party?"

John sighed. "Yeah, despite the danger, a couple of the guys do still go out fishing. I'll tell them to keep an eye out. If you can think of a way of attracting your people's attention that doesn't involve magic—which would probably also attract the creature—then let me know."

"I'll think about it some more, but I know my friend, Jetty, watches the one who takes his boat far from shore. I teased her about it. You could tell him to try calling her name and mentioning me. She might respond."

"All right. I'll tell him. Meanwhile, you rest up and heal. I'll call if there's any news of your people." John turned his attention to Jack. "You're off the duty roster for now. I'll have the other guys fill in."

"Thanks, John." Jack rose to shake the Alpha's hand and walk him to the door.

While they were in the other room, Grace took stock. The Alpha bear was certainly a lot different than she'd expected. In fact, these bears were nothing like she'd thought they'd be.

They were much warmer… friendlier…than she would have believed. For such ferocious creatures, they were really more like teddy bears than the man-eaters she'd seen fishing near the shore.

Oh, she knew they were deadly when riled. So was she. But they were also men with occupations, sensitivity and compassion. She could respect that.

In fact, she found herself almost irresistibly drawn to her rescuer, Jack. He was handsome, to be sure, but he was also kind and caring.

He'd been willing to take a risk to help her, and that counted for a lot in her books. He was also sexy as all get out, and it had been far too long since she'd been involved with a man.

Could a land shifter and a mer mix? She had no idea, but she definitely wanted to give it a try…if Jack was willing.

CHAPTER FIVE

Jack was really happy with the outcome of the meeting. John had gone farther than Jack had expected, going out on a limb to offer sanctuary to any mer needing it. That was a big step, and showed John was willing to take a risk if it might help save innocent lives.

But then, John was a good guy. Half the reason they'd all chosen to follow him as Alpha was because they could count on him when times were tough.

He'd never leave a man behind. And he wouldn't turn his back on someone who needed help.

Jack returned to the kitchen to find his mermaid practically nodding off in her soup. Poor girl was tired.

No. Tired wasn't the word for it. She was exhausted. Running out of gas as he watched her.

"Probably time for you to go back to bed," he said, stepping to her side.

She looked up at him, and he could see the dark circles under her pretty eyes.

"You're right. I think I've been running on adrenaline for the past ten minutes. I was a little...uh...apprehensive about meeting your Alpha." She sat back in her chair and brushed her hair back from her face. "I'm glad he turned out to be such a nice guy."

Jack had to laugh.

"Oh yeah, Big John's a regular ol' teddy bear. You should see him with a grenade launcher in his hands."

She giggled, and he found the sound enchanting. His inner bear wanted to rub up against her and hear the sound again. The beast inside him was fast becoming attached to the mermaid, and Jack wasn't sure whether to be overjoyed at finding a woman his finicky bear actually liked and wanted, or afraid that he was about to have his heart broken by a fickle fish who wouldn't stay on land.

Wasn't that the way all those old stories ended? The mermaid swims off, leaving her broken-hearted lover on the shore. Jack feared very much that's how he was going to end up, but for the life of him, he couldn't stop thinking about being with her—giving a relationship with her a try.

And Jack wasn't the kind of guy who'd ever thought about having a *relationship* with a woman. He was very much a love 'em and leave 'em sort of bear, never sticking with one female for more than a few days or weeks at a time. The moment they started to get clingy, he was gone, his bear roaring to be free.

But not with Grace. Something about her made his inner bear want to be around her. She brought out his protective instincts, for sure. That was a given, considering how he'd found her.

There was more, though. A lot more. Every moment he was in her company, the attraction seemed to escalate, morphing into something a lot more complicated than simple attraction.

She lurched forward in her chair and then

staggered to her feet. Jack put his hands out to steady her.

"Are you sure you can make it back to the bedroom?" he asked, truly concerned for her welfare. She didn't look as strong as she had only a few minutes before, which was to say, she looked weak as a kitten.

"Uh...actually...I'm not too sure."

That was all he had to hear. He stepped closer and scooped her into his arms.

"Hang on, honey," he told her, loving the feel of her in his arms.

She placed her arms around his neck, and something inside him roared in triumph. She was leaning against him, her head on his shoulder, and he didn't ever want to let her go.

Whoa. Those were some heavy thoughts, right there.

He tried not to think about what it might mean while he walked out of the kitchen and down the hall to the guest room he'd put at her disposal.

He placed her gently on the edge of the bed. He let her feet dangle off the side and sat next to her, his arm still around her shoulder, helping prop her up.

"Do you want to make a pit stop or shall

we just tuck you in again?"

"I'm okay for now. How about we just sit and talk for a minute?" He was surprised by her request, but willing to do whatever she liked.

"I can do that." He left his arm around her, and she didn't object, which satisfied him on some primal level. "What's on your mind?"

She tilted her head to look up at him. "I want to know more about your people. About you. I know very little about other kinds of shifters—especially the land-based ones."

Was she flirting with him? Nah. That was probably just his wishful thinking.

"What do you want to know?"

"Do you hibernate in the winter?"

She waited a beat, then burst out laughing, and he liked the teasing light in her eye.

"Considering it's officially winter right now, you're lucky I don't." He laughed along with her for a moment. "Although…I've heard that if you live more in your fur than your skin, some shifters can live among their wild brethren. Mostly they're sad stories where someone loses a mate or their family,

BIANCA D'ARC

or some other emotional disaster, and they shift and stay that way for months on end, living wild. In that case, the animal side takes over, protecting the human side. I think if that happened to a bear shifter, and it happened to be winter, he might seek a nice warm den to hibernate away the coldest days. I mean, wouldn't you?"

"Well, when you put it that way…" She followed his change in mood from playful to contemplative. "Losing a mate must be awful. I could see where staying in your fur would be preferable to facing the human world without your lover by your side."

"We, like most other shifters, mate for life. Once we find our mates, we don't like to be away from them for any length of time." The mood between them changed again. It was suddenly more…intimate.

"It's like that for us too," she whispered.

She leaned into him, her face raised to his so perfectly. He couldn't resist.

He lowered his lips to hers and was immediately swept up in the most devastating encounter he had ever experienced. Devastating because it rocked his world off its foundations and made him rethink what he'd thought his future might hold.

No human woman could feel this good in his arms or taste so sweet. No shifter woman had ever knocked his socks off like this with a mere kiss.

The mermaid, however… She changed his perceptions of reality and reformed his ideas into something more magical than he had ever contemplated.

It was like their energies met and sparked off each other, then settled into a swirling dance of opposites that…attracted. Definitely attracted.

The moment the energy settled down, he pulled her fully into his arms and deepened the kiss. Each new level of intimacy was met with little tingles and a sizzle that eventually settled down into a delicious buzz between them, which heightened every response and drove him onward.

His hands stroked her back, smoothing her long hair. She was so beautiful. He'd thought so from the moment she'd awakened and looked at him with those deep blue eyes. He could happily drown in those eyes and never regret it.

If she let him.

He was very aware of the fact that she

was a mermaid. All the old legends about such creatures ended in heartache for the man foolish enough to fall in love with one. Occasionally, the mermaid herself was left broken-hearted too. Either way, none of those old stories ended happily.

It would be up to both of them to see if they could give their personal story a happy ending. For his part, now that he'd tasted her lips and sampled the way their energies collided, then meshed into something stronger and deliciously appealing...

Well, he was on board. He would pursue her and try his best to make her fall in love with him.

The proverbial ball, as it were, was in her court. He—and his bear—were pretty much convinced that they could make a go of it together, if she gave them a chance.

The bear wasn't saying *mate* just yet, but it was awfully close. Jack could feel his inner bear's conflict. He wanted her to be the one, but he knew this woman was unlike any other they had ever encountered. This woman would not be taken or told. She had to be wooed, and she had to consciously choose him.

Asking her to live on land with him

would be asking her to give up a lot. He would also have to trust that when she did go to the sea, she would come back to him.

That kind of relationship took time to develop. Jack was usually a patient man, but with Grace in his arms, he knew his patience wasn't going to last long. Perhaps he could seduce her into the initial stages of agreement.

No. That didn't feel right.

If they were going to do this, they had to start off on the firm foundation of honesty, not seduction.

Using all his willpower, Jack eased off on the kiss, pulling back and letting her go by small degrees. But he didn't let her go far. He kept his arm around her, supporting her, feeling her warmth as he looked deep into her eyes.

"I've been wanting to do that all night," he admitted, starting as he meant to go on—with honesty between them.

"What if I told you, I'd been thinking about it too?" she asked shyly, giving him a little Mona Lisa smile that nearly melted his socks.

He felt his bear stirring as a satisfied growl sounded in his chest. The bear did that sometimes. He watched her reaction carefully.

Was she disgusted that his animal was so close to the surface?

Grace's delicate hand rose to his chest, landing over his heart. "I like that sound," she whispered. "I like that you're not human. And I like the way our magics dance with each other."

"That's a nice way of describing it. I've never felt anything like that before. You?"

He promised himself he was going to try his best not to be jealous if she'd experienced this all before with some loser who'd let her go.

But she shook her head, and his heart lifted.

"No, that was definitely unique. And kind of exciting." Her shoulders quirked as a tiny smile returned to her face. "What do you think it means?"

Jack sighed and lowered his forehead to rest lightly against hers.

"I think it means that we're compatible, sweetheart. *More* than compatible. Our magics like each other. I wonder if our beast sides could get along? Is there even a way to find out?"

"Bears swim, don't they?"

"We do," he agreed. "But the cove is off limits right now. Don't you need water to shift?"

She nodded slowly. "I do, but it doesn't have to be salt water. Is there a swimming pool in town?"

"Not in town, but my neighbor has one. It's not large, but he uses it for therapy. It's one of those wave pools where he can swim against the current." Jack lifted his forehead away from her. "He was injured pretty bad in the Middle East last time our unit was there. Takes a lot to mess up a shifter."

"Do you think he'd mind if I used it tomorrow? Shifting will help heal me a lot faster. I'd attempt it tonight, but I'm a little too tired. I think it'd be better after a few hours sleep."

"I'll call him. I don't think he'd mind. We can probably go over there tomorrow afternoon."

Jack was already thinking ahead to what he'd need to do to secure his friend's agreement. Georgio could be temperamental since the roadside bomb that had almost killed him.

But Jack knew how to approach him.

Hell, they'd been best friends for a long time.

"Okay. So I'll shift tomorrow, heal up, and you can see how your bear reacts to a mer up close. For tonight, I'm sorry to say, I have to sleep. I'm fading fast here, not that I didn't enjoy the little zip of energy I just got from the way our magics meshed, but it's not enough to keep me running. Sorry."

She yawned, and he let her go a little more.

He had to content himself with the progress he'd already made tonight. This morning, he hadn't even known mermaids really existed, and tonight, he was halfway to trying to convince one to share the rest of his life with him.

Maybe he was pushing this just a little too fast. Or maybe not. Shifters usually knew a lot faster than humans about matters of the heart—or so he'd always been told. He wondered if mermaids were the same.

In a way, he was really looking forward to finding out all the little things about mermaids—and Grace, in particular—that made them tick. He could make learning about Grace his life's work, and he wouldn't mind in the least. In fact, he couldn't think of a more fascinating subject. Or a more beautiful one.

He stood, helping her settle down into the bed with economical motions. She was so lithe, yet so muscular. But then, she'd have to have strength to propel herself through the water.

Those sleek lines helped her slice through the waves the way his much bulkier musculature helped him live off the land in his bear form. They each had aspects of their shifted bodies carry through to their human forms.

They had that in common. They might not be the same kind of shifter, but they were both shifters. They could make this work.

He hoped.

Tomorrow would tell a large part of the story. If their beasts got along, then maybe the human halves would have a chance. Of course, the opposite was also true. If their beasts hated each other on sight, they wouldn't have a prayer. Best to know sooner, rather than later.

He tucked her in and kissed her forehead, stroking her hair gently.

"Rest easy, my little mermaid." He grinned at her as she yawned again. She was losing energy fast, and he moved back as she drifted off to sleep.

CHAPTER SIX

"Moment of truth," Grace muttered as she lowered her legs into the water.

She was sitting on the edge of the small wave pool at Georgio's house. It was midafternoon, but the badly scarred shifter looked like he'd been sleeping when Jack and she had driven up in Jack's SUV. Georgio had a bad limp and lots of scars, but his demeanor had been curious toward her rather than hostile.

In fact, Jack had asked her if she minded if Georgio saw her in her shifted form. Upon reflection, the idea seemed to bother Jack a lot more than it bothered her. She'd agreed, and Jack had laid down some stipulations about how he wanted to give her time alone first—well, with Jack to supervise, in case she needed help—before he'd allow Georgio a glimpse of the real live mermaid who wanted to use his pool to shift.

She just let Jack do what he wanted. She could smell the water, and her skin prickled as her scales itched to come out. Her fishy half wanted to swim, and it would not be denied.

Pleased to learn that there were no chemicals in the water of any kind, she dunked her toe in, watching the scales ripple over her human skin as it began to glow. She put her feet side by side and felt the tingle of magic as her legs formed into the tail that propelled her so efficiently through the water.

She had shed her clothes—some sweats borrowed from Jack that were way too big on her—moments before and sat naked on the rim of the small pool. Her hair was down, and it covered the essentials. When she shifted, she wouldn't feel naked anymore. The protective scales would form a tough skin that hid her human characteristics well enough, and her fish side didn't really understand the concept of nudity.

It knew hunting and playing, friend and foe. Whether it would see Jack as the former, rather than the latter, remained to be seen. All she had to do was shift and let the primal side of her have control for a bit. It would heal her wounds the rest of the way, and it would get a gander at the male who was so very attractive to her human side.

Any minute now...

She slid the rest of the way into the pool and let herself sink to the bottom. Her gills formed as her scales developed, and in the blink of an eye, she was breathing underwater. Her fish side had arrived, and she wiggled her tail, working out the kinks from her recent injuries.

The shift to mer form had gone a long way in healing her. The shift back to human would probably do the rest of the job. For now, she wanted to try out this odd little pool the shifter who lived here seemed to like. She'd never seen one of these therapy pools before, and she was looking forward to trying it out. Though, to be honest, she didn't think it would be able to keep up with her. She'd probably have to temper her pace.

A shadow loomed over the edge of the

pool. Jack.

Her mer form was cautious about anything from up top, but her human side knew it was Jack and rejoiced. The mer side was reserving judgment for the moment.

She pushed up to the top, breaking the surface of the water, her hair streaming down her back.

"How are you doing?" Jack asked.

"Feels good," she told him. "Can you turn on the current now? I want to try it out."

"Sure thing." Jack moved around to the control panel at the front of the pool and hit a few buttons. Jets came on under the water, and she smiled when she felt the stirrings of the current. It was more than she'd expected.

"Is that as high as it goes?"

"That's in the middle. I figured you could work your way through the various settings, if you wanted. Remember, you're just out of your sick bed." He frowned a bit, and her heart melted at the fact that he was worried about her.

"But I feel so much better already," she assured him. "This was definitely the right thing to do. My mer side is happy now, and the magic of the shift took away most of the injuries."

"Most?" he repeated, clearly concerned. "Not all?"

"Don't worry. The shift back will do the rest. For now, I want to swim a bit and work out the kinks."

"Go for it. I'll be right here, and if you want me to up the speed, just stick your thumb out of the water. Point it up for more speed and down for less, okay?"

"Perfect," she told him, already moving away to set herself up in the middle of the current.

Humans probably stayed on the surface to breathe, but she dove down a few feet, testing the different levels of the current, learning its shape and speed. She rose and stuck her thumb up each time she wanted him to raise the speed.

Her mer side was definitely warming to him. It liked the way he worked with her. He would be a good hunting partner, which was what mattered most to her at times when she was mer. He would also be good for play, she thought. He was attentive and kind, playful and knew how to temper his great strength with compassion. He would be a good companion in the ocean, if he were mer.

But he wasn't.

And that stymied the mer side a bit. It didn't know what to make of a man who couldn't swim by her side. Unless...

She rose up to the surface and swam lazily against the current. She'd been right. The speed of the water was a bit slow for her, but after her injuries, it was just right. This therapy pool turned out to be good for injured mer as well as injured humans. Imagine that?

"How long can you hold your breath as a bear?" she asked Jack out of the blue.

"Not as long as you," he answered with a slow, sexy smile. "But way longer than a human."

"I don't hold my breath." She splashed playfully in his direction.

"Then you really do have gills?" He was looking her over as if trying to locate where they were.

"Didn't you see me in mer form when I washed up on shore?" she had to ask.

"Not really. You were shifting when I found you. Glowing. I think it was the magic of your scales fading into your skin. I saw your tail, but I didn't see any gills."

"They're hard to spot," she allowed. She lifted her hair away slightly, turning a little so he could see the small gills located just above her ribs on her sides.

Her mer side felt flirty all of a sudden. It definitely liked the spark of warmth in his brown eyes. It liked his sleek muscles too. And his wit. It weighed and measured what she had learned about him in the short time they'd been together and came up with a favorable review.

The fish half liked him. Imagine that.

Jack wanted to dive into the small pool and take her into his arms. She was as beautiful to him in her mer form as she was in her human skin. The spark of laughter and intelligence in her lovely blue eyes made him want to be close to her. And her magic rubbed against his, warming and welcoming instead of repelling, which was a really good thing.

He had a theory that they were becoming more compatible the longer they spent in each other's company. Their magics were getting used to one another, aligning—much as he wanted their bodies to align in passion and the explosive magic of being together.

He wouldn't wait long after she was healed to press his suit. He'd seen her first, and he wasn't about to let any other bears catch her eye while she was in Grizzly Cove. He wanted to stake a claim in the most emphatic—and pleasurable—terms. If only she felt the same way...

"Mind if I join you?" In true independent bear fashion, Georgio hadn't waited to be invited. He limped into the pool area, leaning on a cane that Jack knew housed a very sharp, very lethal blade inside its carved wooden shell.

"Not at all," Grace answered, smiling at the other man. Jack wanted to growl. Her smiles were supposed to be for him, not some other bear. But she didn't know that yet. Jack had to suppress his possessive tendencies until he'd made his claim, or risk scaring—or more likely, pissing—her off.

"How's the pool working out for you?" Georgio asked politely as he approached.

"It's great," Grace replied, then flicked her tail out of the water. "See?"

Georgio stopped short. "I wouldn't have believed it if I wasn't seeing it with my own eyes. You really are a mermaid."

She smiled, but Jack could tell she felt a

little uncomfortable with Georgio's scrutiny. Still, she was being a good sport about it.

"If it's okay, I'd like to swim a bit more," she said. "This pool really is lovely."

"Be my guest," Georgio replied, sounding more courteous than Jack had ever heard.

With a flip of her tail, Grace went back below water, swimming lazily against the fast current. Georgio came up beside Jack, his gaze trained on the mermaid in his pool.

"She really swims just like a fish," he murmured, watching her as if mesmerized.

Jack said nothing, simply watching the graceful way she moved through the water. She really was named appropriately. Jack had never met a more graceful woman—up to and including the Russian ballerina he'd briefly had a fling with while on a protection detail in Moscow some years back.

"Did you put this pool in yourself?" Jack turned, asking his friend and neighbor. That started a discussion about the pool itself. Jack took mental notes, thinking already about building something like this on his property.

If he was going to be entertaining mermaids—or at least, one in particular—he wanted to make his place comfortable for them. He could also put in a much larger swimming pool, but he had figured the ocean was close enough to swim in when he'd built his home. Now, though, that there was so much danger lurking in the ocean…

He started thinking about where he could put a pool, not just for Grace, but because he liked to swim too. He missed his dips in the ocean.

Although it was pretty clear Georgio would stay in the pool area all day to watch the visiting mermaid, Jack realized, at some point, Grace would want to get out and shift back to her human form. Her *naked* human form. When that happened, Jack's inner bear would go nuts if another male was around to witness it. Jack started guiding Georgio back into the house, promising to help with gathering refreshments and cajoling him into *giving the lady some time alone.*

Georgio was a good guy and took the hint. He also started looking at Jack with suspicion. Well-founded suspicion, Jack knew, but he wasn't about to reveal his attraction to the mermaid to anyone but her. Georgio would just have to go on speculating. At least for now.

If, and when, the time came that Jack was

able to fully claim Grace as his mate—and he still didn't know how that would work with her being mer and all—then everyone would know. He'd be proud to introduce her to his Clan as his mate.

Jack helped Georgio set out some snacks and drinks, including a tall pitcher of pure water for Grace, if she wanted it. They sat comfortably in Georgio's living room, but Jack kept one ear tuned to Grace's movements in the pool. He could hear her splash as she got out and the tiny rustle of her clothing as she dressed.

A few moments later, she joined them in the living room, her hair damp and her shoulders relaxed. She looked tired, but happy.

"How are you feeling?" Jack stood when she entered the room and ushered her to the chair right next to his.

"I think the worst of it is healed now. All that's left is to rest up a bit and regain my strength. The swim, and the shifts, did the trick." She leaned around Jack to catch Georgio's eye. "Thank you again for the use of your pool."

Georgio waved away her thanks with a casual smile. "Happy to help," he murmured before lifting his beer and taking a long sip.

CHAPTER SEVEN

Jack was happy to leave Georgio's. The guy was a friend, and Jack had every sympathy for the badly injured shifter, but Jack found he didn't want to share Grace just yet. He wanted to keep her to himself and secure their relationship—whatever that turned out to be—before they hung out with any more of the Clan.

He parked his Game Warden SUV around the side of the house, and Grace opened her own door, hopping down before he could even get out of the driver's seat. He followed her around to the back of the house, where she stood on his deck, leaning against the railing, looking out at the ocean.

She looked so wistful he wanted to go up and put his arm around her. He wanted to pull her back against his chest and offer his warmth to her. But he wasn't sure where he stood, exactly, so he tread lightly.

"Storm's brewing out there," he said, standing at her side, watching the waves with her.

He'd built the house and deck high enough so he had an unobstructed view of the ocean, while still being quite a distance from the rocky beach. A set of stairs led down from the other side of the deck to the ground. From there, it was a bit of a walk to the ocean, through the tree line and then onto the sandy soil before hitting the actual beach.

"Can you feel it?" Grace's voice was soft as she stared out at the building waves. "Something is stirring."

Jack didn't like the sound of that. And he didn't like the look in her eye either. A change of topic was in order. He put one arm across her shoulders and turned her toward the house.

"How about some dinner? I bet you worked up an appetite with all that swimming and shifting."

She looked up at him as if only just seeing him. Then she smiled, and he forgot any worries he might've had.

"Sure. I haven't cooked on land in a long time, but if you'll help me, I might be able to repay your kindness by trying to prepare a meal. Do you have any red meat?"

He laughed. "Red meat? I thought for sure you were going to ask for fish." They began walking toward the back door, leaving the ocean, and the building storm, behind.

"Fish is better raw, when I'm in my mer form. On land, I like steak. Or a nice, juicy hamburger with all the fixings." Her tinkling laughter rolled over him, drowning him in fairy dust that felt like heaven. She had an almost intoxicating effect on him.

"A girl after my own heart," Jack commented as they entered the house.

He led her right to the kitchen, and together, they began to prepare dinner. Days were short this time of year, and they'd spent hours at Georgio's.

They laughed and enjoyed each other's company as the sun set on the turbulent waters outside. Grace was in good spirits. Her color was better, and she moved with an ease she hadn't been feeling before. Jack watched her carefully for any sign of discomfort, but found none. The swimming and shifting had done the trick. She was in good shape, if still a bit weaker than usual.

Jack understood that. He'd been injured enough to know how shifting could heal a wound, but it didn't really replace the energy being wounded took out of a person. Only time and rest could do that. Jack vowed he'd give her the space to heal, and then, if she was receptive, he'd do his best to court her.

He'd have to probe delicately to learn her people's beliefs about mating. He had to be cautious, just in case it was impossible for them to be together for some arcane reason. But everything inside him was pointing to the fact that she might just be The One.

All through dinner and then after, when they were making small talk before heading to bed, Grace was fighting the compulsion rising in her. She always felt drawn to the water. That was her mer side, wanting to go back where it was comfortable. But this, she feared, was more…

Yet, she couldn't articulate what it was that had her skin itching to feel the cool, welcome mist of the sea on her skin, and the ultimate peaceful immersion in the briny waves. She wanted it so much her mouth was dry. She kept drinking the delicious clear water Jack provided, but it wasn't enough. The ocean was calling her, and she felt compelled to answer.

Compelled. That was something new. Always before, the choice had been hers to make, whether to stay in her skin on land or embrace the waves and allow her scaled form to take dominion over their shared body.

She was yawning for the third time when Jack stood up from the couch he'd been sitting on as they talked quietly in the living room. The entire house was beautiful, showing touches of his artistic talent in the furnishings, the colors and the design.

"You're tired. You've had a big day. Why don't we call it a night?" His tone was gentle, his voice kind.

"I'm sorry. I feel so much better after the swim, but I *am* tired," she admitted.

"I understand. It's the same for me after an injury. The pain and wounds might be gone, but the effects of the energy drain linger."

She nodded, pleased to know they had that in common too. The more they had talked, the more she realized they weren't all that much different, after all. He might be a land dweller, but he was still a shifter, and they had many common traits shared by all shifters.

She stood, stretching her back a bit as she looked at him. She felt so comfortable around him after only knowing him a short while. There was something…

She couldn't decide what to call it. Attraction was too mild. Familiarity wasn't quite right either. There was something sort of…fateful…she felt when he was near. Like they'd done this before in another life. Like they'd spent lifetimes together in another dimension.

She knew it was a little crazy, but that's how she felt. It was inexplicable. She'd seldom had such fanciful thoughts before, but then again, the mer side of her knew it was right. It had decided, finally, that *he* was right. Right for her. Right for both sides of her nature.

But she was too tired to do anything about it tonight. Rest first. Then she would explore these feelings more. Tomorrow.

When she was strong enough to deal with the consequences of giving in to the attraction—and acting on it.

"I'm going to have an early night. Sorry I'm not better company. You've been kindness itself to take me in and help me get back on my feet," she told him.

"Don't mention it," he told her, smiling softly. "It's the least I could do. I'm just glad I was there when you needed me."

It was on the tip of her tongue to ask what would happen if she told him she needed him all the time, but she counseled herself to patience. She was still too beat to start anything tonight. Instead, she reached up and gave him a peck on the cheek before walking toward the guest room he'd given her.

"Goodnight, Jack," she whispered, knowing he would hear.

"Sleep tight," he replied just as softly, and she felt the reverberations of his voice against her sensitive skin like a caress. It didn't always work on land, but her whole body could feel the vibrations in water. That her body was responding so wholeheartedly to him meant something profound.

Tomorrow. She'd deal with it all

tomorrow.

In the middle of night, Jack woke. Something wasn't right. Some noise had awakened him. A noise that didn't belong.

Reaching for his side arm, he crept out of bed and headed for the hallway. The moment he hit it, he felt the breeze that should have been safely locked outside. The door to the deck was wide open, and he could just make out the fleeting glimpse of a white shirt exiting.

His white shirt. On Grace's slender body. She had walked out into the storm in nothing but his shirt, leaving the door to the deck open. What was she doing?

Jack padded out after her, leaving his weapon behind. He was wearing only the boxer shorts he'd put on because she was in the house. Normally, he didn't much care for pajamas or any sort of covering when he slept. That preference went all the way back to when he was a cub and he'd slept in his fur more often than not. Nothing like wearing your own fur coat—it beat a measly blanket any day.

He walked outside to find her just disappearing down the stairs that led into the tree line…and ultimately the beach. Was she going down to the water despite the danger? He had to at least talk to her before he let her go. Even as his heart fractured a little, he went after her, putting some speed on to catch up with her. He had to try to convince her to stay, no matter how much it hurt his pride. He couldn't let her go without at least asking—maybe even begging—her to stay.

"Grace?" he called, approaching her from behind. They were both being pelted with rain, lightning flashes getting closer as the storm grew. She didn't seem to hear him. "Grace!"

Was she ignoring him? He tried again.

"Grace!"

Jack felt a chill that wasn't from the rain. Something else was going on. It looked like her feet were dragging along the ground. Her scales were rippling over her skin, trying to burst out, but unable while she walked toward what could very well be her doom.

As if her doom were calling her.

Sweet Mother of All.

"Grace!" He ran to catch up. She was moving surprisingly fast along the wet sand. They'd made it through the trees and were getting close to the rocky shore.

Jack jumped in front of her, blocking her forward movement. She tried to go around him, but he grasped her arms, stilling her. She kept trying to move, and he saw the pain of struggle on her face. He couldn't tell with the rain streaming down on them, but he thought maybe she was crying.

"Grace, what is it? What are you doing?"

"It's...calling me. It's...compelling me" she ground out, every word a trial.

"The leviathan?" he asked, already sure of the answer. She nodded. "What can I do?"

"It's a little better when you talk to me." Her words seemed to come easier, and she was looking into his eyes now, instead of at the crashing waves just a few yards away. "I felt it pulling me all night. It was building until...until I couldn't resist it anymore."

As a bear shifter, Jack had more magic than most other kinds of shifters, and he recognized the abrasive feel of evil magic against his senses. It was coming from the water, and it was aimed at Grace.

He hadn't made a study of magic the way some of his friends had, but a lot of it just came naturally to him. He had the notion that only stronger, more pure magic, could counteract the evil coming off the water.

Jack's mere presence blocking some of it was already helping steady Grace, but he needed more. *They* needed more.

He wondered if...

Jack bent and kissed her, taking her into his arms, giving into the desire that had been riding him for hours now. There was nothing purer on earth than the magic of desire...the enchantment of love.

He could feel a shell of protective magic forming around them as the kiss deepened. Grace wasn't pushing him away. On the contrary, she was pulling him closer, wrapping herself around him as if he was her anchor in a storm-tossed sea.

Reminded of the dangerous tempest behind him, Jack started walking them slowly back toward the tree line. He didn't stop kissing her. He didn't let her out of his embrace at all. In fact, when he grew impatient with their slow pace, he lifted her off the ground completely and walked at his own pace into the trees.

He felt the rage against his back, beyond the barrier of magic they had created between them. The evil thing in the water was pissed, but Jack would give it no satisfaction this night.

He finally had Grace in his arms, and she responded to him as if she, too, had been dreaming of this. If she had, so much the better. He wasn't going to let her go tonight. Not when he knew she was being drawn against her will.

If he had to hold her in his arms all through the night, then so be it. If, however, things progressed, and she wanted him as much as he wanted her—which it looked very much like it was the case—then he'd take her to his bed and keep her there for as long as she let him. Hopefully, forever.

CHAPTER EIGHT

Jack kissed like a dream. A very hot, very erotic dream.

She clung to him as he lifted her in his arms. He had her around the waist, and she was his willing accomplice as she wrapped her legs around him. His hands moved to support her butt, and she felt chills of delight run down her spine. She loved the way he touched her. Gentle, yet powerful. Masculine, firm and knowing. It was a heady combination.

He was so strong. She felt him walking her up the stairs, carrying her as if she weighed nothing at all. Kissing her the entire time, moving from her lips to her neck, making her shiver even more as her nerve endings came alive for him.

Rain soaked them both, but she didn't care. The slashing water only brought her mer side in alignment with her human side, and both wanted him.

Her body was on an exquisite peak somewhere between her mer scales and her human form, and for the first time in her life, she wanted to make love with a man with both parts of her soul.

Never before had her scales rippled for a male. Never had her body heated so quickly, demanded satisfaction so readily. She wanted him, and she wanted him now.

His skin was slick and hot beneath her hands, and she finally realized that he was mostly naked. He'd come after her in only a pair of boxer shorts that were now wet and clinging to every sexy line of him. She nibbled on his ear as he kissed her neck.

"Make love to me, Jack," she whispered in his ear.

He stopped walking.

"Are you still being drawn?"

She had to laugh. "Yes, but not to the water. I'm drawn to you, Jack. Please tell me you feel it too. I've wanted you almost from the moment I woke up in your guest room. I was instantly attracted, and it's only gotten more potent the longer I'm around you."

"Goddess!" he whispered, seeming overcome for a moment. "I feel the same, Grace. I want you. My bear wants you. All of me wants all of you. But if we do this...it could mean forever. Are you prepared for that?"

Forever? Really? She hadn't thought beyond the satisfaction her body was demanding with every breath. But as the word rolled around in her thoughts, she realized it was a nice word. A comforting word. Not scary at all. Forever.

Yeah, she could easily see spending forever with this special man, held safe in his arms.

"You know? I don't think I'd mind." She pulled back to look into his eyes. "Would you?"

Rain poured down between them, but she could see every nuance of expression on his face and in his gaze. And what she saw there stole her breath.

Emotion.

Deep emotion. Echoes of the yearning

she felt inside her own soul.

There was no way she could walk away from him now without at least finding out if they truly were meant to be together forever. Mates.

Stars above. She might have found her mate, but only taking that final step would tell her for certain.

"Make love to me, Jack. Right here. Right now. Let's find out what fate has in store for us both." She turned it into a dare, but she was breathless with longing, desperate for his possession. She couldn't wait, and she didn't want him to deny her. She needed him. Couldn't he see that?

Jack looked into her eyes for another long moment, then seemed to come to a decision. He didn't speak. He just moved toward the nearby railing, setting her butt down on the wide rail. She was naked beneath his shirt, so the only thing that had been separating them was his soaked boxer shorts.

"Are you steady up there?" he asked, waiting for her to put her hands on the rail on either side. When she nodded, he stepped just a few inches away so he could remove the nearly transparent, no-nonsense white cotton that did little to conceal the long, thick hardness of him.

And then, the offending fabric was gone. In a wad on the deck beneath his feet. And he was gloriously nude. A statue of a Greek god come to life before her.

She reached between them and took him in her hand. She felt the slight shudder run through him as she squeezed lightly. The cold rain and wind did nothing to diminish him. He was better than every hot fantasy she'd ever entertained, and she didn't want to wait.

Tugging him forward, she scooted closer. Since he was such a tall man, the deck rail was the perfect height, but she needed his cooperation to get what she desired. Her perch was too precarious to do it all herself.

"Come into me now," she plead with him, her voice thick with yearning.

"Are you sure?" He cupped her cheek and looked deep into her eyes. "Last chance to back out."

"I don't want to back out." She squeezed him gently once more. "I want you."

"Then what am I waiting for?" He smiled at her as he stepped closer. She had to loosen her hold, guiding him to her core. He pushed forward slowly, holding her gaze as he began to fill her.

He felt amazing. Truly wonderful. Absolutely delicious. And big.

Oh, yeah.

His hands went to her ass, and then, he began to move. He had a tight hold of her, and she felt safer than she ever had with any man, even as she sat on a slick wooden railing fifteen feet above the ground. Rain poured over then as he came into her fully, over and over again.

He pumped slowly at first, letting her get accustomed to the feel of him. And then, when her body was straining for more, he gave it to her. Hard, fast, and just the way she needed it, he pounded into her.

She heard herself moaning and crying out. No man had ever wrung such a response from her before. She was wild in his arms. As wild as the night and the storm that raged around them. Magic welled up between them again, blocking out everything around them. Only the two of them existed in the bubble of their magic and the passion of their joining.

That's when she knew. He was her mate. Her magic wouldn't rise like this for just anyone.

Not only did their magics mesh and form a protective bubble around them, but they joined and built upon each other. She felt the weight of worry lift off her shoulders as her mind finally understood what her body had been trying to tell her.

Jack was her mate.

That thought was the last clear notion she had as he rocked into her, sending her senses into orbit with a few nearly out of control final thrusts. She screamed as she came, clawing his back and making him growl. She loved the way the sexy sound heightened her pleasure, the rumble in his body acting like a vibrator everywhere they touched.

Jack couldn't help himself. He growled as he came, his bear half acknowledging the woman as his mate. This was it. He finally knew for sure.

Grace was his mate.

Goddess help him if she thought otherwise. Then again, she seemed to have been with him every step of the way, even going so far as to ask him for what she wanted when he would have waited to initiate deeper intimacy between them. She was a woman who knew what she wanted, and he hoped like hell it turned out that she wanted him. Forever.

He carried her back inside after they'd both taken a moment to catch their breath. The bubble of magic around them had dissipated, and they were both wet from the slashing rain. He left puddles on the floor he would think about later as he carried her straight to the master bath.

She wasn't shivering. Her mer side must keep her warm in cold water. So he just took a moment to dry them both with a couple of fluffy towels before lifting her once again into his arms and taking her into his bedroom.

Grace was almost asleep, allowing him to move her around without comment as her eyes drifted closed. She was still recovering, and the little sojourn out into the storm hadn't helped. He tucked her into his bed and climbed in beside her. He took her into his arms and fell asleep with a smile on his face.

Twice in the night, she grew restless as the storm raged against the house. It was as if the creature out there in the dark was expressing its anger through the harsh weather. Both times, Jack held her, and her discomfort subsided. She didn't try to leave the bed, and Jack hoped the simple, miraculous action of making love had severed the hold the leviathan had seemed to have on her earlier.

Each time, she woke, and they made love. The affirmation of their desire seemed to banish all the negativity coming off the ocean. And the pleasure was like nothing he'd ever had with any other woman. If he'd known finding his mate would result in that sort of ecstasy, he would've begun searching for her a lot sooner.

But the Goddess worked in mysterious ways. Jack was a big believer in fate. He thought maybe Grace had washed up on his beach exactly when she was meant to, and all the searching in the world wouldn't have brought them together any sooner. They had to meet when they were both ready.

Boy, was he ready.

He wanted what his brother had. A mate to love and a home to be proud of. He'd built the latter, and he'd just discovered the former. He was one lucky son of a bitch.

Now all they had to do was deal with the sea monster on his doorstep, and all would be well. Tall order, he knew, but he'd tackled more difficult tasks in his life. He, along with his brothers-in-arms, would make it happen. They had to.

CHAPTER NINE

Jack was gone from the bed when Grace woke the next day. She'd slept really late. She could tell by the slant of the sun behind the blinds that it was closer to noon than dawn. She sat up and pushed her hair back from her face. She could tell it was a tangled mess. Between the rain and going to bed with it damp—and then the restless sleep and all the incredible sex…

Oh, yeah. She'd had sex with Jack. If she'd been a cat, she would have purred remembering the pleasure he'd given her. Her mate.

A sense of wonder passed over her. She'd found her mate. Now *that* was really something. A momentous occasion. A life-altering event.

But did he feel the same? A little niggle of doubt crawled into her mind. And then, she remembered how the storm had raged with evil anger and how the sea had called to her even in her sleep. Jack had been there to calm her and break the spell, but she'd still felt drawn to the ocean in a way that wasn't normal, or good.

In the cold light of day, she felt miserable about that. What if it grew so strong that she tried to leave him again? She couldn't bear that. Not now that she knew he was her mate.

Her heart was his. She cared so much for him, and yet, even now, she could feel the pull of the evil thing out there in the water. She wanted to cry. How could she be both so happy and so scared at the same time?

Happiness was Jack. Finding him was a miracle. Fear was that thing out there. It wanted to devour her, steal her magic and swallow her whole.

One positive note was, now that she and Jack had made love, the call wasn't quite as strong. Either their joining had somehow weakened the connection between her and the thing that had almost killed her, or—

more worryingly—it could be that the creature was laying low for the moment, lulling her into a false sense of security.

But she didn't feel secure. Not at all. That thing was still out there, and she could feel it stalking her.

She got up and took a warm shower, taming her hair and relieving the little aches and pains that came from the unaccustomed activity of the night before. She smiled to herself, enjoying the memories of what they had done together. Jack was such a good man, and a considerate lover.

"I hope that smile is for me."

Jack's voice came to her from the doorway of the bathroom. Her eyes opened, and she met his gaze through the slight mist of steam from her shower. The curtain was open just enough for her to see him.

"You bet it is," she told him as he strolled into the room, shutting the door behind him, shutting the steam inside the room with them. She loved the feel of the warm mist on her skin. It was a sensual delight—almost like being embraced by water, even on land.

He stood before her in just a pair of jeans. The top button was open, and he looked so sexy she wanted to lick him from head to toe.

"I just wanted to check on you. How are you feeling?" His gaze narrowed in concern.

"I feel fine. Great, in fact." A smoldering look passed between them.

"What me to check for splinters?"

"What?" His comment threw her. What in the world was he talking about?

He moved closer, standing right up near the shower curtain.

"From the deck rail," he said. It took her a moment to register. "I apologize if that first time was a little rough."

"I liked it," she assured him, smiling now, her mood restored. "And I don't think I have any splinters."

"You sure? I'd really like to check." Apparently, he was in a playful mood.

"I just bet you would."

He raised his hand and grasped one edge of the shower curtain, near her face. His expression turned serious.

"You do things to me, honey. Things I've never felt before," he told her.

"Good things?" He was so serious, for a moment, she was worried he wasn't happy with the change in their relationship. Her stomach clenched.

"The best," he whispered, dipping his head to place a light kiss on her lips.

Her heart started beating again. In fact, it sped up as his lips touched hers. It was just a peck, really, but it was a sign of affection she hadn't expected. She could get used to this sort of thing—having a mate around who bestowed exciting little kisses on her throughout the day, and even better things at night…or whenever. It would be easy to become addicted to him.

He pulled back while she was still tingling and thinking happy, sensuous thoughts.

"Now are you ready to come out of there, or do I have to come in after you?"

She smiled her invitation, and he pushed the curtain aside in one quick motion. He stepped into the shower, jeans and all, though they weren't on him for very long. He closed the curtain again, enveloping them in the intimate, steamy atmosphere as he took her into his arms.

What followed was a sexy, water-slick exploration. A coming home. A reunion of hearts—she hoped—and bodies that had become very well acquainted last night. But they wanted more. Body and mind, she wanted much more of this man. So much, it might take a lifetime to get her fill.

Shower sex was awesome as far as Jack was concerned. Then again, any sex with Grace was awesome. Like, truly epic.

After they were both dry and dressed—at least partially—again, he served breakfast in the kitchen. There were some things he really needed to know about his little mermaid, and he hoped to get some answers.

Over eggs and bacon, he started asking questions.

"What is mating all about for your people?" He knew the question wasn't very subtle, but she didn't seem to mind. She smiled at him and answered between bites of breakfast.

"When a mer finds a true mate, they share their magic. It's a partnership on the magical level that can never be severed." Her voice had grown serious as she spoke.

"True matings on land are like that too, except for the magic thing. I mean, I assume there's some kind of magical bond as well, but since most land-based shifters don't have conscious control over their magic, it's more an instinctual thing for us." He chewed for a moment before asking more questions.

"How do mates integrate their magic? Do you have mage-craft under the sea?"

"There are some who weave spells underwater, but not many. Mates retreat to one of Neptune's holy places deep in the ocean, and something magical happens there that joins them forever. Nobody really knows exactly what happens, except for the couples who've been through it, and they don't ever give any details. It's all a big mystery, but then, we have many of those in the ocean."

"Hmm." Jack was thinking through the difficulties. "Obviously, I can't go deep into the ocean without special gear, so that won't work for us." He heard her breath catch, and he had to smile.

"You mean...?" She looked so hopeful, something in his heart lifted.

"You're my mate, Grace. If you feel the same, I'd like to figure out a way that we can be together forever. What do you say?"

She jumped out of her chair and landed in his lap, hugging him around the shoulders as she pressed kisses to his face. Now that was the kind of response he'd been hoping for.

"Oh, Jack," she whispered between kisses. "You're my mate."

Those words made him growl in pleasure.

He would have taken things farther, but she sat up, a worried frown on her face.

"What's wrong?" His low words brought her attention back to him.

"What if the leviathan lures me away again?" Her whisper was full of fear. He stroked her back, trying to soothe her, but he could feel the tension—the terror—in her quivering muscles.

"It won't." He tried to reassure her.

"But last night…" Her eyes filled with tears. "If you hadn't been there to hold me back, I don't know what would have happened. I still feel the pull of it. Only your presence stops me from answering."

"That bad?" Things were worse than he'd realized.

He'd thought after that initial problem last night, when he'd brought her back from the beach, it had been over. Or at least, more manageable. He didn't like thinking that the call was still so strong.

She nodded, and one tear tracked its way down her cheek. He kissed it away, feeling a tenderness come over him that he'd never felt before.

"I love you, Grace."

His quiet words astounded him. Her, too, it appeared, from the way she was blinking at him, her eyes wide with surprise.

"I…I…" She seemed to stumble over her own tongue for a moment, and his heart skipped a beat. Was she going to deny him? Repulse his feelings? He held his breath as she finally seemed able to speak. "I love you too."

Jack could breathe again. She loved him. She *loved* him!

"Thank the Goddess for that," he whispered, sealing his words with a deep, lingering kiss that spoke of joy and of love.

When he finally let her up for air, she rested her forehead against his.

"What are we going to do? I'm so afraid I'll leave you. I don't ever want to leave you, but I can't be with you every single moment of the day. What if, in some unguarded moment, the call becomes too strong?"

Jack could see the very real fear in her eyes, the worry in her words. He had to fix this for her. For them. They needed to do something that would make her feel safer— that would keep her safer. There had to be a way.

"This is a magical problem, and although

I'm more magical than most shifters, I'm no expert on this kind of thing, but…" He looked deep into her eyes. "I do have a friend who knows about this stuff. He's a special kind of bear, and he's a trained shaman. He lives just down the coast a short distance. He's part of our group, but he also serves the Native American community to the south. He lives with one foot in both worlds and is the most magical, spiritual person I know. If anyone can help us, I believe he can."

Hope dawned in her eyes for the first time. "Do you think he'll help us?"

"Honey, that's what he does. Ol' Gus was the unofficial chaplain in our old unit. Since then, he's become a counselor to troubled youth on the Indian reservation. He's a good guy. He'll help if he can."

"When can we see him?" Her eagerness both delighted and concerned him. Was the call of the evil that strong?

"I'll give him a call." She slipped off his lap, and he unclipped his cell phone from his hip, punching in the number. "Luckily, he's back from his trip to the east coast. He went for some extra training or something, but he's back now."

CHAPTER TEN

Gustav van Wilde was a mystical man, Grace thought. He had an otherworldliness about him that both enchanted and set her at ease. Such was the way of the shaman, or so she'd been told. His gray-blue eyes were spooky, almost see-through, and it felt like they looked beyond the surface, right into her soul.

He'd come right out to Jack's house after he'd called for help, which meant Gus was a good friend to her mate. She could feel the concern coming from Gus as Jack filled him in on their problem. Gus asked a few questions, then sat back and seemed to think the problem through. She liked that. He was very deliberate and didn't rush into things that could impact the rest of their lives.

"I can help you merge your magics," Gus said after a good long think. "You have to be certain though, because once done, this cannot be undone. Are you both absolutely sure you're true mates?"

Grace nodded and saw Jack do the same. She knew he was her one and only. She would never love another the way her heart yearned for him. It was common for her people to fall in love quickly with their true mate. Such was the way of things in her world. She was glad to learn it was the same for the land-based shifters.

After Jack had confirmed that little fact, she hadn't doubted his commitment. They were the same in so many ways. And now, their hearts were aligned too. The ways they differed didn't matter so much in light of that. They'd figure it out.

That left only their magic...

"Will it stop me from answering the call?" She had to ask. "Or will it make us both susceptible? I don't want to put Jack in danger."

Jack covered her hand with his. They were seated side by side on the couch while Gus sat in the easy chair across from them.

"If this goes as I think it will, it should do both. Jack might feel the call to some extent, but with your combined magic, you should both be strong enough to deny it. By sharing in Jack's magic, you'll feel more connected to the land, and he might be more attracted to the water because of you, but you'll both be stronger together than either of you are alone." He shrugged. "You would have discovered this truth on your own, given enough time together. Mating is a merging, and it happens over time. What I propose to do is speed up the process."

"Sounds good to me," Jack said, squeezing her hand reassuringly. "When can we do it?"

*

Gus took them up near his place to perform the ceremony. He'd built his home on a rocky stretch of land near the southern tip of the cove. He had a large spread that bordered the shifter lands on the north and the Native reservation to the south.

There was a small stone circle up on a bluff that faced the ocean, which was why the shaman had wanted this particular piece of land. Such formations were sacred to the Goddess, and Jack knew they were natural places of power. Jack counted it as a blessing to know this place was here, so close to their new town and his own property.

"Has the energy settled down any more?" he asked Gus as they approached the stone circle. It was a low-profile formation, but it was definitely a power place. Jack could feel the magic and the welcoming feeling of the energy.

Gus shrugged as they kept walking. "Big John told me all about how the altar came to be. I'm working with his new mate to try to tame the power a bit more. It's still pretty wild, but when I get a better grip on it, and my role in our new community, I hope to make this a gathering place for our people. A ceremonial place. But I need a little time to figure it all out. Right now, the power here is still somewhat untamed. It's very new. The magic is strong, and in its formative stages here. It's like starting from scratch."

"Are you sure it's safe to do this here?" Jack halted, forcing the other two to stop and look at him. Grace was at his side, her hand in his. Gus was in front, turning back to look at them both.

"Yes," he stated calmly. "I'm certain it'll be okay for this. There's only three of us, and the process is relatively simple. I'm just nudging something along that is already in progress. It can't hurt you. I'm just not sure how the wild magic of this place will respond to a large gathering of bears. We're very magical in our own right, and if the place isn't prepared for the influx of power, the results could be a little unpredictable. I want to be sure I've got the circle used to our brand of magic before I invite the whole town up here."

Jack was still skeptical.

"Look, I promise you'll be safe. When have I ever steered you wrong?"

Jack had to admit Gus had always been true blue. He'd never done anything that would make Jack doubt him, but this time, it wasn't just Jack's neck on the line. He turned to Grace.

"What do you think?" Part of being mated was having a partner, and Jack intended to start as he meant to go on, asking Grace for her input on the important decisions that affected them both.

"I can feel the goodness of the place," she said, looking toward the stone circle. "It repels the evil in the ocean. Already, the call is diminished to almost nothing."

"It'll be gone the minute you step into the circle," Gus promised.

"I can't believe anything could harm us there," Grace said. "We have places like this on the ocean floor. Places sacred to Neptune and his servants. If that's what this is, then I think we should go ahead. It'll work out as fate demands."

"Interesting perspective," Gus mused. "When this is all over, I'd love to talk to you about your people's beliefs, if you're willing."

Grace looked surprised, but pleased by Gus's interest. But that wasn't getting them anywhere. They had a decision to make.

"Look," Gus said, seeing Jack's obvious reluctance. "Come into the circle. Get a feel for it and see what you think." Without waiting for an answer, Gus started walking again, heading directly for the nearest standing stone.

"Are you really okay with this?" Jack asked Grace once more before making any sort of move.

"Yeah, I think it'll be okay. I'm getting a good feeling from the place. You'll see." She reached up and cupped his cheek. "And just for the record, I love it that you're so careful of my safety." She kissed him briefly, then turned and started walking, tugging him by the hand after her. She was headed for the stone circle.

Sure enough, Jack felt at peace the moment he stepped inside. Gus, as usual, had been right. Nothing evil could get to them here.

The power of the place tasted almost feral though. Strong and untamed. But benevolent in its own way. It had matured a bit since the last time Jack had been up here with John and his new mate, when she'd set the last of the permanent magical wards that now protected the cove.

"Can you feel it?" Grace turned to him, wonder in her eyes.

He rumbled a reply while Gus went around to the four compass points, chanting something under his breath. Jack wasn't too concerned. He'd seen his friend do that sort of thing many times, in many places. Gus was the guy all the shifters in their unit went to when they had spiritual or magical problems, which were often one and the same.

Since they'd come to Grizzly Cove,

though, Gus had been out of sight much of the time. He hadn't really been involved with the creation of the town, preferring to build ties with the Native peoples just to the south. And then, he'd gone back east, to Long Island, seeking counsel from a Native medicine woman. Big John had sanctioned both moves. It was only smart to have someone interface with the closest group of humans, and Gus was the logical choice because of his spiritual leanings, and all knowledge was useful. Getting extra training was something John always supported in anyone under his command.

In general, the bear shifters meshed well with the Native Americans of the area, and Gus's very nature seemed to earn their respect. Gus was a special kind of bear. Rare and revered in this part of the world. He'd been born and raised in British Columbia, Jack knew, and he'd been eager to settle in the Pacific Northwest when Big John had suggested it, even though most of Gus's immediate family was gone.

"Are you both ready?" Gus was finished with his prayers and had turned back to Jack and Grace.

Jack looked at Grace, and she gazed back

at him.

"What do you want us to do?" she asked, keeping her attention focused on Jack and Jack alone. He liked that. So did his inner bear. He stepped closer to her and took both of her hands in his as they stood near the stone altar at the center of the circle of stones.

"That's perfect, actually," Gus said, sounding bemused. "Just keep holding hands like that and don't let go. I'm going to coax your magics into the open. There's a chance you might feel the exchange. Ideally, they magic will meet, merge, split and remerge, then return to each of you, two halves of one whole. Sound good?"

"Just get on with it, Gus. I want my mate safe."

"Keep your shirt on, Jack. The Goddess doesn't appreciate your impatience, and neither do I."

Grace giggled. The exchange was typical of the camaraderie between Jack and Gus, and the rest of the guys from the old unit, for that matter. He was glad Grace seemed to understand that without being told. She really was perfect for him in every way.

Gus began muttering again, speaking

words in a chanting tone, beseeching the Mother of All and the Great Spirit among others. Jack knew the divine went by many names, and though he called Her the Goddess, he didn't object to other people's beliefs—as long as they were on the right side of things.

Gus chanted a bit more, gesturing with his hands now and then. It took a few moments, but then, all of a sudden, Jack felt it. His spine went rigid as his inner bear roared at the intrusion. It felt like his magic was being sucked out, none too gently.

Jack heard Grace gasp and felt her hands tighten on his. The sensations weren't comfortable. Not at all. But it wasn't exactly painful. Just really, really odd.

And then, there was a cacophony of indescribable sound and a glimmer of golden light mixing with turquoise above their heads. He couldn't look at it. It was too bright. And besides, he wanted to keep his eyes on Grace. Whatever he was feeling, so was she. He could see it in her eyes.

If they just concentrated on each other, they could get through anything. Including this majorly uncomfortable sensation.

The sucking feeling ended, and Jack's

inner bear felt a strong sense of dismay. Jack felt empty. As if every drop of magic in him had been wrung out. Which it probably had.

Jack realized the golden magic was his, mixing with the pure blue of Grace's, somewhere above their heads, inside the sacred circle. Jack hoped Gus would work fast. He'd never been this uncomfortable in his life—including the time he'd been captured by terrorists intent on torturing information out of him. They hadn't succeeded, but it had been a dicey few hours before he'd been able to free himself.

The gold and blue merged into a lovely greenish hue around them, then it split again into gold and blue. And then, it merged again, just like Gus had said. Green light showered around them, bathing them in its glow as the magic began to trickle back into them both.

Was it his imagination, or had the intensity and quantity of the light increased markedly?

Jack started to believe he wasn't dreaming when the power began to come back into him. It started slow and then became a steady stream, building as it returned home, into his soul. It was stronger. There was definitely more of it. And it was…different. It had a salty flavor, if he had to describe it. The light was no longer the gold of the earth alone. Now it was mixed with the blue of the ocean to form something new. A green that tasted of both, and was stronger than either had been alone.

Grace's eyes widened as she discovered the newness of their shared magic about the same time he did. She gripped his hands tightly, but the wonder in her gaze mirrored his own feelings exactly. There was nothing to fear in this. It felt right and good.

Gus had come through for them. He'd joined them closer and faster than they could have done on their own. Jack prayed the boost in power would keep Grace safe from the call of the evil thing in the water. That was the most important thing…her safety.

She was everything to him. His life. His world. His love.

"You're that to me too," Grace whispered, as if she'd been able to read his thoughts.

Had she? It certainly seemed that way. And wasn't that an interesting result of this sharing of magic? Jack wondered if it would be a long-term effect or if it was something momentary that would wear off. Only time would tell.

"I love you, Grace." And he didn't care that Gus could hear him. Everyone should know that she was his and he belonged indelibly to her. They were mates.

She moved into his arms, and they hugged each other tight, each holding the other until the final traces of magic had settled back into their souls. When the broke apart, they were both smiling softly.

A small sound to the right had Jack looking over at Gus. The shaman seemed stunned, clinging to a nearby rock with a dazed expression on his face. Jack frowned.

"Is he okay?" Grace whispered, stepping back, out of Jack's embrace.

"Not sure," Jack answered, already moving toward his friend. "Hey, buddy, you all right?"

Gus blinked a few times, trying to focus on Jack. He was out of it, no doubt, but he looked like he was coming around. Jack hadn't realized this work would take so much out of the shaman. Jack touched Gus's shoulder, and a little shock zinged through him and then was gone. Residual charge from the intense magic that had been flying around the circle only moments before?

"Did you see it?" Gus's raspy voice garnered Jack's full attention.

"The light? I didn't look directly at it, but I saw the colors change. It's green now. Pretty cool. And it feels nice, like it belongs. As if it's always been this way. I didn't expect that." Jack helped Gus stand up straight, still concerned for his friend.

"There was a message in the light," Gus claimed, his voice still weak. "A vision. I saw mermaids in the cove."

"Swimming?" Grace asked, a smile on her lips.

"Swimming and walking the streets. Your people were part of our community," Gus confirmed.

"Wow." Grace looked from Gus to Jack and back, clearly surprised by Gus's words.

"I like that idea," Jack voted. "I'm just not sure what the rest of the guys are going to think."

Gus chuckled and it was a happy sound. "I saw young. Little swimmers and little bears. I don't think anyone who finds a mate among the mer will mind at all."

Jack knew the truth of that firsthand.

CHAPTER ELEVEN

When they stepped outside of the sacred circle, Jack felt the pull of the sea. And then, he felt the call of the evil in it. It wasn't strong, but it was persistent. He turned to look at Grace.

"How is it now?"

The relief on her face spoke volumes. "So much less than it was. It's just a light buzz now. Easily ignored. Before it was a siren. I can manage this. No problem."

Relief flooded him as well.

Whatever happened next, they were in this together.

Grace walked beside the two men. Gus had been drained by the work he'd done to help them, but he was able to walk, with a little support from Jack. She liked the way the old comrades leaned on each other, and she particularly liked the shaman and the vision he claimed to have seen. If he was right, she wasn't going to be the only mer in Grizzly Cove.

It was something she'd talked about with her sister when they realized the town was being built in one of their favorite resting spots. Before the bear shifters had claimed the land, the cove and its secluded beaches had been a favorite spot for sunbathing and gossiping. Since the land-dwellers had come, though, her hunting party had stayed clear.

Maybe now, they could all live in harmony, sharing the cove. It was a nice thought.

Her life was here now, because Jack was. He was her mate.

That thought still made her tingle with joy. She finally understood why her mother had chosen to stay on land with her dad. They were true mates, just like Grace and Jack.

He was her safe harbor. He was the link

to the land that kept her in her human form, so they could be together.

It was beautiful, really. And Grace knew from observing the deep love between her parents, that it could work. She couldn't wait to introduce Jack to her folks. Grace thought her mom would be overjoyed that one of her children had found the same incredible happiness she had.

"You know…" Grace heard Gus talking to Jack as they walked slowly down the bluff, "I have a feeling there's more than just mer in Grace's bloodline."

"What do you mean?" Grace went to Gus's other side.

He was moving better now, regaining strength as they got farther away from the stone circle and closer the house in the distance.

"Only one of your parents is mer, right?" Gus asked, instead of answering her question.

She nodded. "My dad is human."

"A little more than just human, I would say." Gus's cryptic words made her frown. "Your sire is probably a mage."

"Dad isn't magical at all," she told him, trying to think of what Gus could possibly be getting at.

The shaman shrugged.

"He's probably latent, but there's mage potential in your energy. It's not solely mer. Even for a mer, you pack a wallop, Grace. Part of that is due to your father. And that magic on his side—in the open, or not— probably has a lot to do with why your parents' mating works so well. Their magic probably blends and complements each other. The magic is the glue that holds them together. And because bears and mer are so innately magical, the signs are good that you two will do really well together too. You're well balanced and will have strong cubs and a bright future."

"More visions, Gus?" Jack challenged his friend with a broad smile. "Or wishful thinking?"

Gus tilted his head to one side as if considering.

"A bit of both, actually. If I didn't say it before, I'm really happy for you and wish you nothing but the best in life. You deserve it."

Jack sobered, reaching out to hug his buddy, pounding his back a couple of times. "Thanks, Gus."

When they broke apart, Gus sobered. They had stopped walking and were surrounded by tall sequoia, birds flitting around them in the forest. It was an idyllic place.

"I feel it's only fair to warn you though..." Gus's expression was troubled. "We're in for a rough ride. That thing is still out there, and Goddess knows what else is happening in the greater battle against evil. My biggest fear is that the leviathan is a symptom of something far worse."

Grace saw Jack's jaw firm, and his spine went a little straighter. He wasn't going to cower in fear.

He was going to fight.

And if that was the case, she'd be right there with him, fighting at his side. She was a huntress, not a minnow. Her new mate would learn that soon enough—as would the rest of the members of her new community in Grizzly Cove.

"Your lady and her people will be effective allies, if what I've foreseen comes to pass. They'll be the first line of defense against enemies who would approach from the sea—and you're part of that now, Jack. The blending of your magic makes you uniquely qualified among the bear population. You'll learn the way of it in time."

"Do we really have that kind of time?" Jack asked in a low voice.

Gus sighed. His expression darkened for a moment.

"We'll be dealing with this problem for some time to come. I wish I could say differently, but from all I've seen and surmised, you'll have time to figure out the new magic and will be called upon to use it at some point in the future. You know what to do. Learn it as quick and as well as you can. Get ready. Be prepared."

Jack nodded. "I'll be a regular boy scout."

Gus clapped him on the shoulder, then turned to look at Grace.

"You'll both have a role in this. Between the two of you, you'll have responsibilities toward both the land and the sea. The Mother of All wouldn't have joined you— blessed you—so completely, if She didn't have plans for your unique talents." Gus cracked a smile.

Grace smiled back at him. "I'm a huntress, which means I'm part of a group— what we call a hunting party—that protects and defends the bigger gatherings. We also hunt to provide for ourselves and our people," she told them, noting the way both men's eyes widened. Well. She was glad she could surprise them. Being underestimated was one of her best tactics. "It's in my nature to do the same here on land as I do in the ocean. And if my sisters are allowed to swim in the cove once again, they'll do the same. We protect. It's what we do."

Gus looked at her, then shifted his gaze to Jack, merriment dancing in his eyes. Jack seemed just as amused, but she didn't feel they were laughing at her.

"I want to be there when Big John finds out the mermaid has teeth," Gus said cryptically.

"The rest of the guys are about to get a huge wake-up call," Jack agreed, folding his arms in front of his chest as if in satisfaction. "Here we all thought we were the big badass defenders of the cove, and it turns out we're going to have help from fierce, beautiful women." Jack unfolded his arms and put them around Grace's waist, pulling her in for a playful hug.

"Grizzly Cove will never be the same," Gus agreed, chuckling.

"Maybe that's a good thing." Grace kissed her bear, knowing her world had definitely changed...for the better.

# # #

EXCERPT:
BEARLIEST CATCH
Grizzly Cove #6

Drew popped open a beer after setting his lines and sat back in his favorite deck chair to enjoy the sunrise. He'd motored out while it was still dark, being careful to keep his magical shield up and running at all times. He didn't want to end up as a snack for the creature that haunted the depths out here, but he had to be out on the ocean when his internal demons came home to roost, as they had that night.

Nightmares often drove him out, onto his boat, in the middle of the night. He was lucky that fishermen often set sail before dawn. None of his buddies really knew how bad he was. He'd been able to hide it from them so far. But alone on the ocean, he could forget his troubles and just…be.

Except…somebody was staring at him. Dammit. He'd felt this a few times before, but dismissed it. Now, of course, he thought he knew who it was.

A few days ago, a half-dead mermaid had washed up on shore and his friend Jack, who had taken on the role of game warden, had found her. He'd nursed her back to health and the Goddess must have been at work, because they had discovered a mutual attraction that turned out to be another true mating.

The mer were some of the most mysterious of all shifters. Not much was known about them, but Jack's new mate— her name was Grace—had been revealing little bits here and there. One of the things they'd told Drew in particular, was that Grace's hunting party might be looking for her, and that one mer in particular, a gal named Jetty, might have occasion to swim near his boat from time to time.

Grace had asked him to make contact with her friend, if at all possible, to let her people know that she was all right and staying on land for the time being, with her mate. John had gone one farther and told him to deliver an even greater message. He'd offered the mer asylum in the cove while the leviathan prowled off shore.

That was a big step, and Drew knew it. Inviting another group of shifters into their territory was monumental, and impressed upon everyone how dire the situation with the sea monster really was. Not that they didn't know already. Everyone had seen the thing attacking Ursula when she'd cast it out of the cove with her powerful, magical wards.

It was like something out of a horror flick. Massive. Multi-tentacled. And so evil, it reeked.

Drew was able to sense the creature and its minions to some degree, and was able to avoid areas where he believed they were lurking. Part of his magic, in addition to shielding, was sensing danger—and when he was being observed.

Like right now.

"Hey mermaid, if you're the one called Jetty, I have a message for you," he called out.

He'd never tried to talk to her before. Of course, he hadn't really been sure what—or, in this case, who—was watching him before.

He'd thought maybe it was a dolphin or something. He hadn't sensed any malevolence from the presence, just a sort of neutral curiosity that didn't really set off his spidey senses for danger.

He figured now that he had some intel on who was watching him from the water, he'd try the direct approach. If that didn't work, maybe he'd dive in and swim around with the fishes for a bit. See if that got any response.

Though, of course, it was dangerous to go swimming with something that could breathe underwater when you couldn't. He'd be a little nuts to do it, but Drew liked to live dangerously. If he didn't, he'd have stayed safe in the cove, away from the sea monster and it's evil children, and curious mer creatures who spied on him for no apparent reason.

He kind of hoped the mer would respond to his direct approach. He'd never seen Grace in her shifted form, and he was really curious about what mer looked like. In human form, Grace was just like any other person, though even Drew had to admit, she was a lovely woman. Jack had lucked out, finding such a beautiful, and nice gal washed up on his beach. The Goddess had truly been smiling on the bastard.

"Your name *is* Jetty, right?" Drew tried again. "Grace told me you like to spy on my boat now and again. She's all right, by the way. She sends her regards. The leviathan cut her up pretty bad, but my friend Jack found her and it turns out they're mates. You missed the ceremony, sorry to say."

"Grace is mated?"

The sultry female voice came to Drew from the port side of his boat. He got up from his chair and approached the rail, peering over slowly so as not to startle the mer woman.

To read more, get your copy of
Bearliest Catch *by Bianca D'Arc.*

ABOUT THE AUTHOR

Bianca D'Arc has run a laboratory, climbed the corporate ladder in the shark-infested streets of lower Manhattan, studied and taught martial arts, and earned the right to put a whole bunch of letters after her name, but she's always enjoyed writing more than any of her other pursuits. She grew up and still lives on Long Island, where she keeps busy with an extensive garden, several aquariums full of very demanding fish, and writing her favorite genres of paranormal, fantasy and sci-fi romance.

Bianca loves to hear from readers and can be reached through Twitter (@BiancaDArc), Facebook (BiancaDArcAuthor) or through the various links on her website.

WELCOME TO THE D'ARC SIDE...
WWW.BIANCADARC.COM

Dragon Knights
(continued)
The Ice Dragon**
Prince of Spies***
Wings of Change
FireDrake
Dragon Storm
Keeper of the Flame
Hidden Dragons
Sea Dragon

Science Fiction Romance

StarLords
Hidden Talent
Talent For Trouble
Shy Talent

Jit'Suku Chronicles ~ Arcana
King of Swords
King of Cups
King of Clubs
King of Stars
End of the Line

Jit'Suku Chronicles ~ Sons of Amber
Angel in the Badlands

Futuristic Erotic Romance

WWW.BIANCADARC.COM